SO, ON THE MORN THEY RODE INTO THE FOREST OF ADVENTURES....
—LE MORTE D'ARTHUR

~

*For Irene and Milo, with much love*

First edition 2012

Library of Congress Cataloging-in-Publication Data is available.
Library of Congress Catalog Card Number 2011046646

ISBN 978-0-7636-5311-8

13 14 15 16 17 CCP 10 9 8 7 6 5 4
Printed in Shenzhen, Guangdong, China

This book was typeset in Caslon Antique.
The illustrations were done in watercolor and ink.

Candlewick Press
99 Dover Street
Somerville, Massachusetts 02144

visit us at www.candlewick.com

# KING ARTHUR'S VERY GREAT GRANDSON

Henry Alfred Grummorson was the great-great-great-great-great-great-great-grandson
of King Arthur, the noblest knight ever to wield a sword. . . .

## Kenneth Kraegel

CANDLEWICK PRESS

ON THE DAY Henry turned six years old, he woke up early,

ate a large breakfast,

mounted his trusty donkey, Knuckles, and went
out in search of adventure.

He had heard of a fire-breathing Dragon lurking far out in the hills, so into the hills he went.

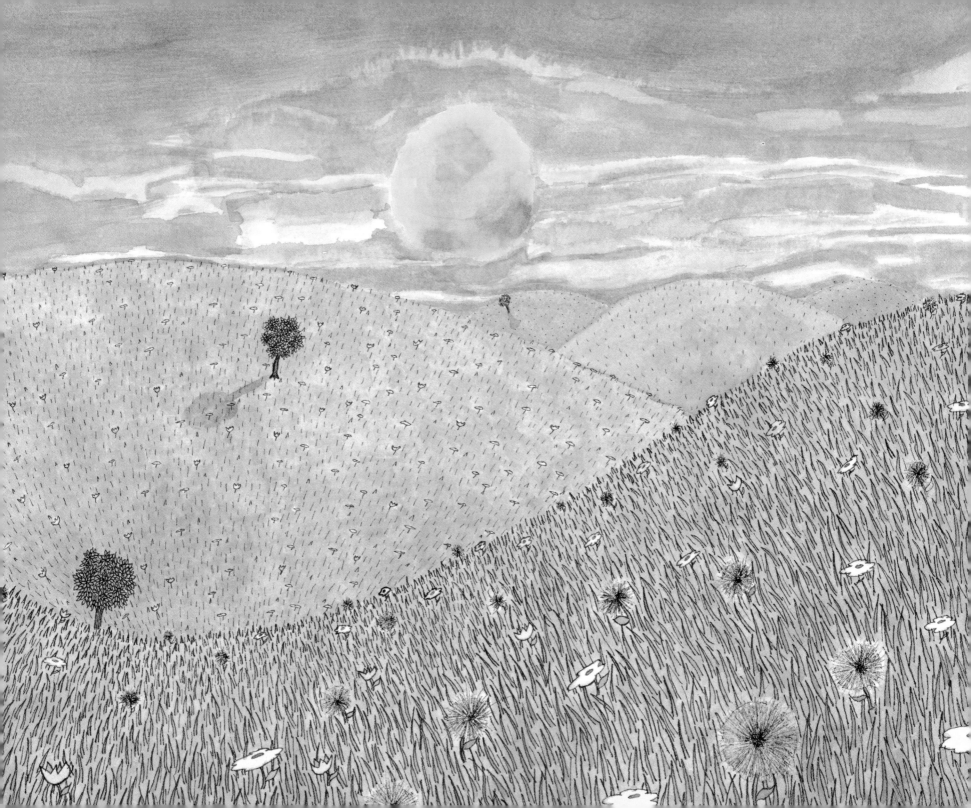

When he found the terrible Dragon, Henry announced himself loudly:

"BEHOLD, VILE WORM!  I, HENRY ALFRED GRUMMORSON, A KNIGHT OF KING ARTHUR'S BLOOD, DO HEREBY CHALLENGE YOU TO A FIGHT TO THE UTTERMOST!"

The Dragon drew in a long, slow breath . . .

but all he blew out was smoke rings.

"Can you top that, young knight?"

"SMOKE RINGS?" Henry exclaimed. "I have no time for smoke rings! I want to fight, strength against strength, might against might!"

"I see. Well, if rough adventure is what you seek, maybe you should try the Cyclops up in the high mountains."

Straightaway, Henry and Knuckles sped into the high mountains, eager to do battle with the one-eyed giant.

Near the day's end, Henry found himself face-to-face with
the dreaded Cyclops.

"GIANT, I AM HERE TO DO BATTLE WITH YOU!
PREPARE YOURSELF, AND LET US BEGIN!"

The Cyclops stared at Henry, and Henry stared back.
They stared and stared until Henry could stare no longer.

"ENOUGH, LONE-EYE!" Henry shouted. "YOU HAVE HAD TIME APLENTY! LET THE BATTLE COMMENCE!"

"But the battle has already begun," the Cyclops explained. "Whoever blinks first is the loser. I thought you understood."

"NO! NO!" cried Henry. "I am not interested in a staring contest. I want a struggle of arms, a test of might and courage!"

"Hmmmm," the Cyclops considered. "If it is physical peril you desire, you should visit the Griffin down in the valley."

Once again Henry and Knuckles were off.
They galloped through the night, eager to do
battle with the ferocious Griffin.

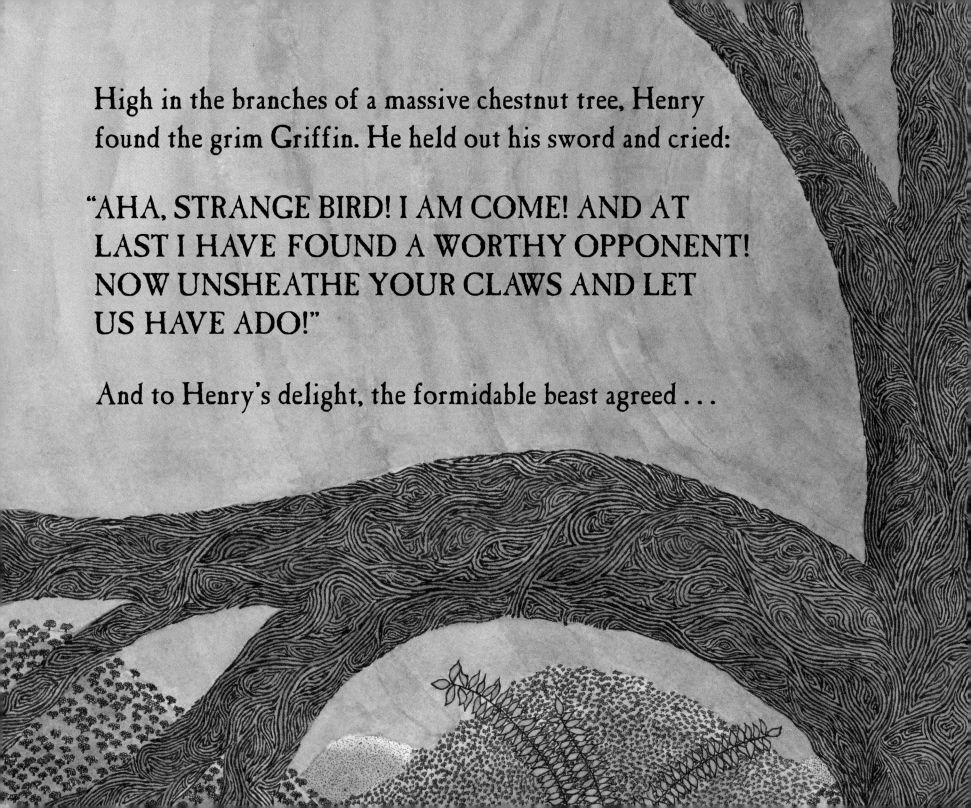

High in the branches of a massive chestnut tree, Henry found the grim Griffin. He held out his sword and cried:

"AHA, STRANGE BIRD! I AM COME! AND AT LAST I HAVE FOUND A WORTHY OPPONENT! NOW UNSHEATHE YOUR CLAWS AND LET US HAVE ADO!"

And to Henry's delight, the formidable beast agreed . . .

and pulled out a chessboard.

"I prefer black. Is that okay?" the Griffin asked.

"NO! IT IS NOT OKAY!" shouted Henry. "I WANT
SWORDPLAY! A STRUGGLE! A BATTLE TO THE
UTTERMOST, AND IF YOU WILL NOT HAVE
ADO WITH ME, TELL ME WHO WILL!"

"Well, if it is danger you seek," advised the Griffin,
"then go down to the sea and you will find the Leviathan.
Of all the living beasts, he is most to be feared."

So Henry leaped atop Knuckles and rode furiously to the sea, determined to have a battle, come what may.

There in the roiling waters, Henry caught a glimpse
of a truly enormous beast just below the surface.
He cleared his throat, gathered together his six years
of manhood, and shouted:

"READY YOURSELF, MONSTER, AND I SHALL HAVE ADO WITH YOU! FOR I AM HENRY ALFRED GRUMMORSON, THE GREAT-GREAT-GREAT-GREAT-GREAT-GREAT-GREAT-GRANDSON OF ARTHUR, KING OF BRITAIN!"

# EEEEEEEEEEEE

I say, grrrreeeetings to the highly esteemed great-great-great-gr—
Hey! Wait! Where are you going? I thought
we were going to play a game? Hello?"

Even though he hadn't subdued the Leviathan, Henry was not dismayed. After all, he had traveled great distances and come face-to-face with four terrible monsters.

To his knowledge, not even the great King Arthur had accomplished as much in his first two days as a six-year-old.

But Henry had also found something he hadn't known
he had been looking for . . .

friendship—and he liked that very much.